First Little Readers™

The Mouse and the Magic Bee

by Liza Charlesworth

ISBN: 978-1-338-29791-1

Illustrated by Tammie Lyon

First printing, June 2018.

Once upon a time,
there was a little mouse.
"I am so boring," he said.
"I do not want to be ME."

BIZZ BUZZ!
A magic bee appeared.
"I can help you," she said.

"Awesome!" said the mouse.
"I want to be pink
like a pig."

"Okay," said the magic bee.
BIZZ BUZZ!
She made the mouse pink
like a pig.

"Awesome!" said the mouse.
"I want to have wings
like a butterfly."

"Okay," said the magic bee.
BIZZ BUZZ!
She gave the mouse wings
like a butterfly.

"Awesome!" said the mouse.
"I want to have a tail
like a peacock."

"Okay," said the magic bee.
BIZZ BUZZ!
She gave the mouse a tail
like a peacock.

"Awesome!" said the mouse.
"I want to be big
like a bear."

"Okay," said the magic bee.
BIZZ BUZZ!
She made the mouse big
like a bear.

"Awesome!" said the mouse.
"Now, I just want a mirror."

"Okay," said the magic bee.
BIZZ BUZZ!
She gave the mouse a mirror.

The mouse took a look.
“NOT awesome!” he squeaked.
“I made a mistake.
I just want to be ME.”

"Okay," said the magic bee.
BIZZ BUZZ!
She made the mouse
a mouse again.

"Awesome!" said the mouse.
"I love being ME!"
And he lived happily ever after.